Henry Holt and Company, LLC
Publishers since 1866
175 Fifth Avenue
New York, New York 10010
www.HenryHoltKids.com

Henry Holt® is a registered trademark of Henry Holt and Company, LLC.
Text copyright © 1991 by Bill Martin Jr
Text copyright © 2004 by the Estate of Bill Martin Jr
Illustrations copyright © 1991 by Eric Carle
All rights reserved.
Distributed in Canada by H. B. Fenn and Company Ltd.

Library of Congress Cataloging-in-Publication Data
Martin, Bill, 1916–2004.
Polar bear, polar bear, what do you hear? / by Bill Martin Jr;
pictures by Eric Carle.
Summary: Zoo animals from polar bear to walrus make their
distinctive sounds for each other, while children imitate the sounds
for the zookeeper.
[1. Animal sounds—Fiction. 2. Zoo animals—Fiction.
3. Stories in rhyme.] I. Carle, Eric, ill. II. Title.
PZ8.3.M4113Po   1991   [E]—dc20   91-13322

ISBN-13: 978-0-8050-8897-7 / ISBN-10: 0-8050-8897-0
First Edition—1991
Printed in the United States of America on acid-free paper. ∞

10 9 8 7 6 5 4 3 2 1

Polar Bear, Polar Bear, What Do You Hear?

By Bill Martin Jr

Pictures by Eric Carle

Henry Holt and Company · New York

Polar Bear, Polar Bear,
what do you hear?

I hear a lion
roaring in my ear.

Lion, Lion,
what do you hear?

I hear a hippopotamus
snorting in my ear.

Hippopotamus, Hippopotamus,
what do you hear?

I hear a flamingo
fluting in my ear.

Flamingo, Flamingo,
what do you hear?

I hear a zebra
braying in my ear.

I hear a boa constrictor
hissing in my ear.

Boa Constrictor, Boa Constrictor,
what do you hear?

I hear an elephant
trumpeting in my ear.

Elephant, Elephant,
what do you hear?

I hear a leopard
snarling in my ear.

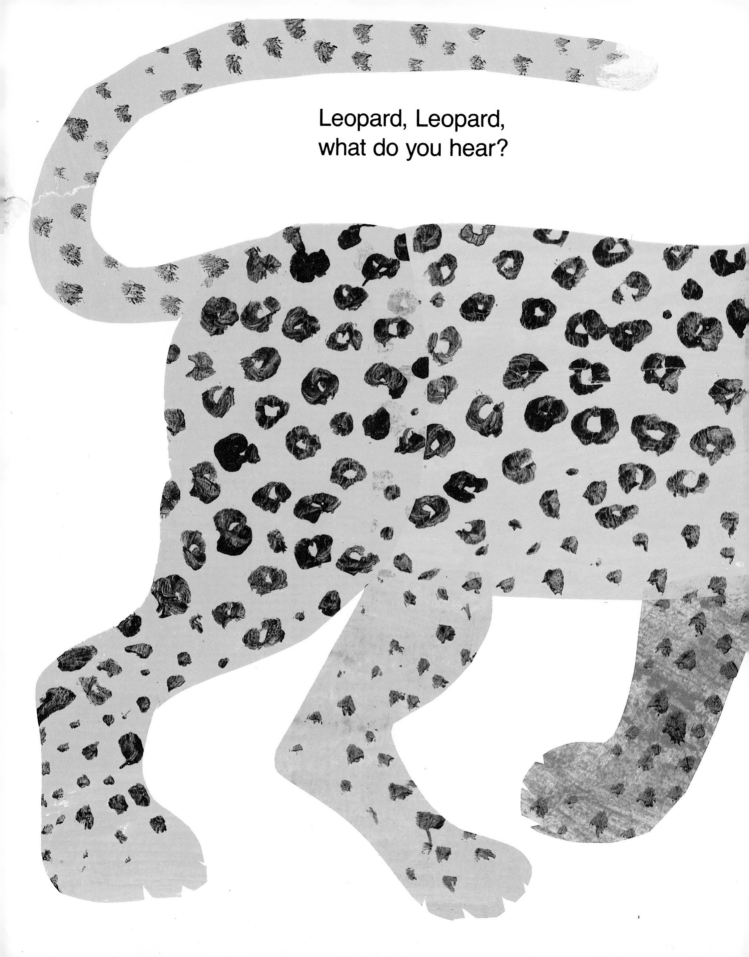

Leopard, Leopard,
what do you hear?

I hear a peacock
yelping in my ear.

Peacock, Peacock,
what do you hear?

I hear a walrus
bellowing in my ear.

Walrus, Walrus,
what do you hear?

I hear a zookeeper
whistling in my ear.

Zookeeper, Zookeeper,
what do you hear?

I hear children . . .

. . . growling like a polar bear,
roaring like a lion,
snorting like a hippopotamus,
fluting like a flamingo,
braying like a zebra,
hissing like a boa constrictor,
trumpeting like an elephant,
snarling like a leopard,
yelping like a peacock,
bellowing like a walrus . . .

that's what I hear.